The Blinkers and the Bolgers

...and other Be Yourself Stories

D1560686

By Jimmy Cennamo & Frank Nagorka

The Blinkers and the Bolgers
...and other Be Yourself Stories
By: Jimmy Cennamo & Frank Nagorka

Book design: Vincent-louis Apruzzese / behemothmedia.com

The Blinkers and the Bolgers

Page 5

The Baldies

Page 23

Miss Manást ... a Secretary

Page 37

The
Blinkers
and the
Bolgers

The Bolgers lived in a big house at 356 Bulky Avenue. It was near the town bakery, ice cream shop, and the hamburger stand.
The Bolger house had three refrigerators and four freezers.
They had a food pantry that was the size of a garage.
The basement of the Bolgers' house looked like a grocery store.
There were aisles of assorted foods.
There were large hams, sausages, doughnuts, cakes, cheese wheels, chocolates, and many bottles of root beer.
The Bolger kitchen smelled like something was cooking all the time.

Boris Bolger and his wife, Betty, had three children.

Their names were Bruce, Bertha, and Boris Junior.

All of them were large.

How could they not be? They loved to eat so much. Betty
Bolger made large meals for breakfast, lunch, and dinner.

She also made cupcakes, ice cream sundaes,
and deviled eggs to snack on.

She basted roasts, she simmered gravy, and she baked
lasagnes. Something was always cooking at the Bolger
household - and being eaten!

This is the family of the Bolgers

The Blinkers lived around the corner from the Bolgers,
at 330 Sliver Street.

Their house was taller and not as wide as the Bolgers.
The Blinkers' house had many plants, bicycles, vacuum
cleaners, and large glass bowls with matchbooks from
different parts of the world.

There were spice racks in the kitchen, but not much
food to spice. The Blinkers' kitchen had a bowl of
apples.

There were cucumbers, lemons, zucchinis, and a jar of
a very spicy sauce in their small refrigerator.

There was a cabinet that held their medicine.

Hugh and Harriet Blinker had two children.

Their names were Henry and Heather.

Everyone in the Blinker family was skinny.

They didn't eat very much. They didn't like to.

They liked to do things like dusting the house, cleaning the closets, and carving little statues in the basement.

The Blinker basement had a large woodworking machine and no food in sight.

The biggest thing about the Blinker family was Harriet Blinker's hair. She was proud of her large curls.

But like the rest of her family, her waist was tiny.

Henry and Heather's legs grew longer, but their waists seemed to stay the same.

This is the family of the Blinkers

The Blinkers and the Bolgers did not like each other. Harriet Blinker pulled down the window shade whenever she saw the Bolgers buying lunch at the hamburger stand. She did not like that they were eating - again! One day, the Blinkers were outside trimming their hedges when the Bolgers walked by with a box from the bakery. It was a cake, the Blinkers just knew it. It was no one's birthday either. The families began arguing. They yelled at each other. "You eat too much!" the Blinkers said. "You eat too little!" said the Bolgers. They made fun of each other. They pointed and began to hurt each other's feelings.

THE Bolgers said,
"You should get some meat on those ribs of yours."

Then the Blinkers said, "You should get some meat OFF those ribs of yours"

15

The time had come when the big mulberry tree in town was covered in ripe, yummy fruit. The Bolgers wanted to pick all the mulberries and make mulberry pie. The Blinkers went to the tree, but they were only picking mulberries for exercise. At first, the families were mean to each other. "You have mulberry all over your face!" Harriet Blinker said to Bertha Bolger. "You have mulberry all over your pants!" Boris Bolger yelled to Hugh Blinker. The day was hot. The mulberries were soft and dripping. Soon, every person in both families was covered in mulberry. Everyone was pink and purple - from head to toe!

The Blinkers and the Bolgers were very bad enemies And this is how they made friends

Sometimes, being yourself happens when you least expect it. After the families went home and took baths, they thought about the reasons they did not like each other. It was because they were different from each other. That's a silly reason, especially when every person, Blinker or Bolger, is sticky with mulberry juice. Bruce Bolger called the Blinkers, and asked if they would like to go to the town ball with him and his wife. "Why not?" the Blinkers said. Everyone dressed up and had fun. When the Bolgers danced, it shook the drinks on the tables. The Blinkers didn't mind, though.

THE Ball

Now the Blinkers and the Bolgers are very good friends. They are having fun twisting at the ball

20

Back home, the kids made popcorn at the Bolgers' because the Blinkers didn't have any popcorn at their house. All four of them fit nicely on the couch, while Boris Junior crawled on the floor. "Do you like butter on your popcorn?" Bruce Bolger asked. Henry and Heather Blinker shrugged. "We'll give it a try," they said. They put the popcorn in the middle of everyone. They watched funny shows on television.
They felt good.
Everyone likes making new friends,
and learning from them.

The Baldies

Concetta and Agnes Baldie lived together
in a small house on a hill.
They were both bald. Their mother and father were bald,
aunts and uncles, and all of their grandparents.
Still, it upset Concetta and Agnes.
They did not want to be bald. They wanted to go out with
the boys, and what boy wants to be seen with a Baldie?
No one called them, and they didn't call anyone. They felt
broken-hearted. The Baldies' telephone was dusty and
covered in spider webs from disuse.

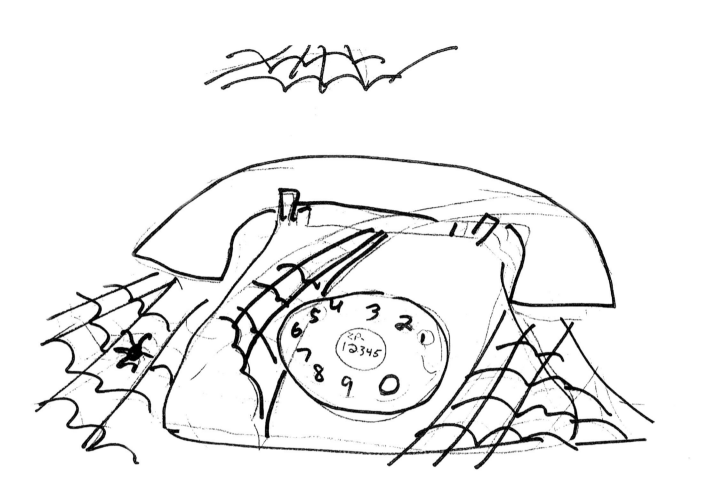

Concheta and Agnes Baldie lived together in a small house upon a hill. They never got a phone call for a date because they were both bald, and

One day at the store, Concetta noticed a tonic called "Hair Grower". She brought it home. She and her sister were so excited, their broken hearts nearly lept out of their chests. They followed the instructions. They rubbed the tonic on their heads. It had to work—the bottle said it was a guarantee. But after the weeks went on, the Baldie hearts became even more broken, still no hair.

The telephone was dustier than ever.

here they are
So how about that?

Notice the hair grower on the table. They used it but it didn't work.
(Boo Hoo Hoo)

The Baldies decided to do something else. They saw a commercial on the television. They wondered why they had never thought of it before. The commercial was for wigs. It was fake hair you put on your head that allowed you to pick any style and color. Short hair, long hair, straight hair, or curly hair—what a dream! They chose what they wanted. They ordered the wigs to be shipped express to the Baldie house.

The wigs came the next day.

Agnes Baldie was now blonde and Concetta was a red head. The wigs were thick. They looked natural! No one would know. The Baldies wondered if they should change their last name. They got dressed up and went out. Two handsome men saw them. They asked for the Baldie's telephone number. Agnes and Concetta were so excited. They cleaned the telephone and waited.

The two men called from their house in the same town. It was a special night. The men asked, "Would you like to go to the amusement park tomorrow?"
"Why, of course!" the Baldies said. Concetta whispered to Agnes. "Don't tell them our last names!"

At the amusement park, the Baldies went on the bumper cars, the Ferris wheel, and they played games.
At the end of the day, they all decided to go on the roller coaster. What a mistake! The Baldies were having so much fun. They had forgotten they were wearing the wigs.
When the roller coaster went down the first big hill, the wigs flew off! The Baldies were in shock.
The handsome men started laughing at them.

At the park they went on the roller coaster and it was going so fast that their wigs fell off

everyone laughed at them

The Baldies were once again broken-hearted. They thought, maybe we should order big hats. But they couldn't wear hats all the time, could they? When they thought about it, you had to take off your hat when you went out to dinner, or went out dancing. The Baldies decided to be themselves, to embrace who they were. They decided not to hide themselves.

Soon, their phone rang again.

Miss Manást
... a Secretary

Miss Manást needed a new job. She found an ad in the newspaper. A man downtown needed a secretary. She took the city bus to the big insurance building where the man worked. The man was very busy. He needed so much help. He hired Miss Manást even though he couldn't remember her name! She was the first person to come for the secretary job. She started working right away.

41

Miss Manást was the plainest girl in town. She was very quiet and very skinny, but she could type fast. Her fingers were the strongest part about her. Sometimes on the city bus, it became very loud and frightened Miss Manást. She read the gossip magazine on the bus, and at her desk when her boss was in a meeting. Miss Manást wondered sometimes what it would be like to be beautiful. Would people treat her differently?

One afternoon, a very rich lady came to buy some insurance. She had on a lot of makeup and she looked beautiful. The lady went into the office.

Miss Manást took out her magazine. There was a girl on the front who looked so happy. Her eyes were bright, her teeth were white, and her boyfriend was handsome. Their smiles were wide. The pages of the magazine were glossy. Everyone had a special life. Everyone was doing something special. It was because they were beautiful. Miss Manást decided to make a decision.

The next day Miss Manást came to work dressed up. She wore gobs of makeup and no glasses. The makeup looked silly because Miss Manást had never worn makeup before. Therefore, she had no idea how to put it on correctly. The high-heeled shoes pinched her feet and made her walk funny. The red dress was so small and tight, Miss Manást could hardly breathe. And how could Miss Manást type? She couldn't see without her glasses! Miss Manást decided to paint her nails at her desk because she couldn't do anything else. She spilled the nail polish on very important papers and documents, and her boss became very angry with her.

Miss Manást was sad and embarrassed. She asked her boss if she could have the afternoon off. She went back to her apartment so she could scrub her face. She changed into her old clothes. She put on her glasses, and the whole world became clear again. Why did she do something that made her something she wasn't?

It only caused problems.

The next day at work her boss said, "You look better plain, Miss Manást." Miss Manást felt much better, and that's what counted. Inside, she was not plain at all.

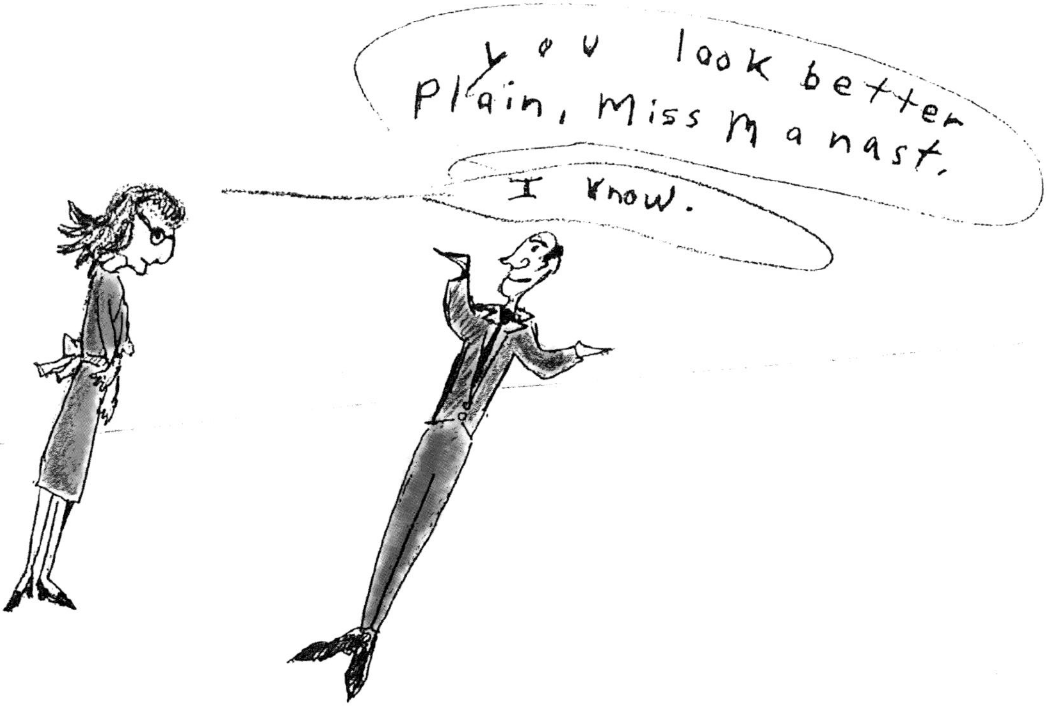

moral of the story
Don't try to be something you aren't

the end.

Frank Nagorka   &   Jimmy Cennamo

Special thanks to Alex Liptak and Krista Osipovitch .

Made in United States
North Haven, CT
19 April 2022